DANGEROUS LOVE

FICTION, YOUNG ADULT, ROMANCE

ANA

Made with ♥ on the Notion Press Platform
www.notionpress.com

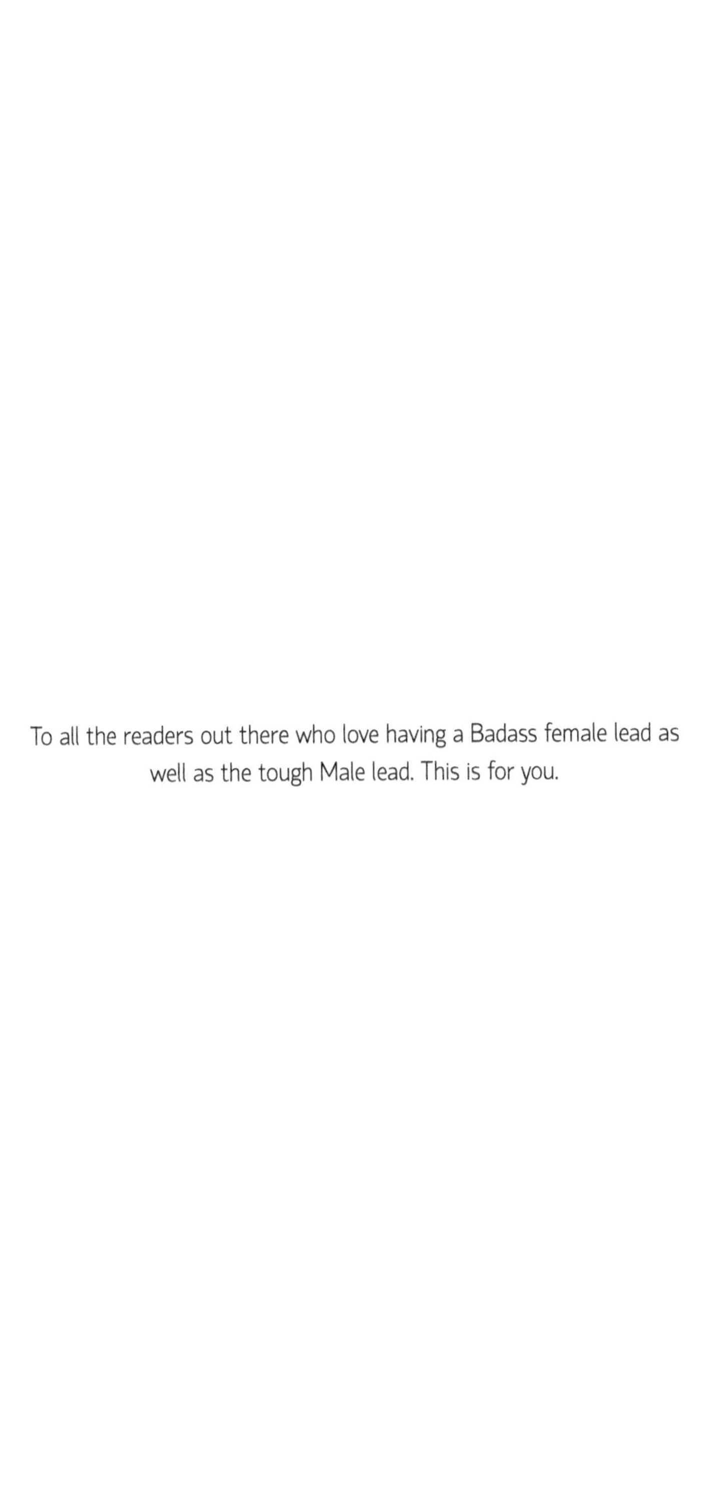

To all the readers out there who love having a Badass female lead as well as the tough Male lead. This is for you.

Contents

Acknowledgements

First of all a big thanks to my parents who didn't know about me writing something until I had written about half of the book. Thanking my friends for their constant support and proofreading my work to find some errors and giving a go on the spicy scenes.

Chapter 1-3

CHAPTER 1

Here I am lounging on a chair in my bikini at a lone island, which is basically a hideout of my brother, with more security than required during constant rounds of the entire island just because some psycho mafia leader, **Roth**, is out for search of my brother and wants to kill him and his any relatives so that he can become the next biggest mafia leader in Asia.

Well I am **Wang Ji Eun**, sister of one of the biggest mafia leaders of Asia, **Ji Wook Wang**. After our father died in some inter clan fight my brother took over his business and became one of the biggest mafia leaders. He loves me the most and thinks that I am as fragile as other girls out there and do not want to understand that I am anything but fragile. I have always seen blood and people being shot in front of me ever since our father was in this business so I am not that affected by blood and seeing people being murdered. As for my safety he has put **Jeon Ji Hyun**, formerly his personal bodyguard, to keep an eye on me and ensure my safety. Honestly he is damn hot and my type, not that I have a particular type but I don't like being watched 24/7. I have often caught him sneaking a few glances towards me here and there but I am not quite sure about it.

My whole life came to a standstill when one day my brother dropped the bomb that we have to pack our bags and go into hiding because Roth is after my and Ji Wook's life. I had to leave my studies in between and flee without uttering a single word to anyone even to my friend they only know that I am on a long vacation. So basically I am bored to my core as I don't have anything to do all day long. As for my brother he is with his girlfriend who he loves very much. Well yesterday when I told my brother about my boredom he said that he will take me to the city as he also wants to see into some of his business, so tomorrow or day after we will be going away from this dreaded island and back to the main city.

I don't have many friends but one is my best mate, Aubrey, she knows everything about me from my first crush, my relationships to the fact that I have a little craze for guns. She also knows the fact that I am on a run with my brother instead of on a vacation. My past relationships were not more than a fling and I didn't have that many relationships because I was the sister of a mafia leader so that used to scare people off of me. I also can't contact her because this island doesn't have any cell reception either so whole day I am either having a sun bath or roaming around the small library in the house my brother built on this island years ago. I plan to meet up with Aubrey once we go into town that if my brother allows me to or if I have the balls to sneak out from his or any of the bodyguards' sight, especially Ji Hyun's because he sticks with me all the time.

My train of thoughts is broken when I hear a deep voice "Ma'am, lunch is almost ready would you like to go in the house now? "Ji Hyun asked. "Sure, let's go". We went inside the house and saw Liza, our housekeeper setting the plates on the table.

During lunch Ji Wook asked Ji Hyun about the security details on the island and about visiting the city to which he answered that it is all set and we can visit the city safely. "Can I go and meet Aubrey in the city?" I asked with my puppy dog eyes, which always worked. My brother hesitated for a moment and then said "You can meet her but as long as you follow JH's security instructions and let him stick with you all the time and don't you dare and try to lose him under any circumstances" he said with threatening eyes and that was my cue to not argue any further. "JH after dropping us off stick with them all the time, no matter what" Ji Wook commanded "Definitely sir" he answered.

I was happy that I get to meet Aubrey after so long and I can't wait to meet her and hear her ranting about how I left her in college all alone and how she got bored every day. I just don't like the fact that she will be meeting Ji Hyun because I know for sure that she will try to make a pass at him which I will not like at all.

CHAPTER 2

JI EUN POV:

We finally came to the city and the first thing I did after getting cell reception is that I called Aubrey to inform her that I am in the city and plan a meet up. She was more excited than me to meet up although she scolded me a lot for leaving all of a sudden.

We were in the limousine with Ji Hyun behind the wheel, me in the passenger seat and Ji Wook in the back with his girlfriend with the privacy glass closed between the back and front seats. I was getting a little uneasy with the awkward silence in the car and also I was giddy to meet my bestie.

I opened the privacy glass and looking back I saw that both my brother's face and his girlfriend's face were flushed and I concluded that they were doing something nasty back there. "At least keep your hands to yourself when you are not alone and have company in a freaking car" I said to which my brother retorted "That's what the privacy glass is for baby sis. What do you want?" he asked. "When can I go to meet Aubrey? And how much time will we have?" His and Ji Hyun's eyes met in the rear view mirror for a moment and then he replied "after Ji Hyun drops us off at the company you can go wherever you want with that friend of yours as long as you follow JH's instructions." "Okay thanks and for your information 'that friend of mine' has a name and it is A-U-B-R-E-Y, Aubrey" I said back. Ji Wook just smirked cause he knows that I get irritated whenever he doesn't remember my friends' name and sometimes he does it on purpose.

After about half an hour they were dropped off at the company, we changed cars and set off to pick Aubrey up from her house and go for shopping and other stuff. My brother gave serious instructions not to wander about. Finally we reached Aubrey's house, I called her to inform her and within minutes she was sitting in the car with us and we were going towards the main market for shopping. As soon as she entered the car she said "hey stranger, where have you been all this time? It seemed like you just vanished into thin air and off from this planet's face. Don't you dare ghost me again" "I was not ghosting you it was just an emergency and besides I told you that I will be going away for the time being" I told her. "Now that you say it I actually remember that you did tell me" she smiled sheepishly and then we talked about random things until we reached the shopping area. We got off and stormed into one of the shops, JH following just behind us, not that close but not that far either. He was looking extra cool in his black aviators with his signature black outfit. As soon as we entered the shop Aubrey asked "Is he going to follow us everywhere we go?" "Yes" I said simply while looking through the clothes. "Can't we lose him some way?" she asked "We can....." I said continuing ".....Unless I want to die" I said with a straight face. She turned me towards her and asked "Do you like him?" I don't know why but I felt my face heat up a little bit and turned away from her to hide my blushing face murmuring a little 'no'. Cocking an eyebrow she asked "Are you sure?" I turned toward her and before I could answer her she said "oh someone's blushing, so yeah I got my answer" and strode away. I walk up to her and said " I don't really know if I have any feelings for him, it's just that he is around me like all day so I got used to his presence around me, that's it."

After sometime she came out of the dressing room wearing a yellow summer dress, and she was looking ravishing in it. She twirled once and asked "How am I looking?" "Fabulous as always babe" I replied. She turned toward me and said "you going to try that dress on or what?" I came out of my daze and dashed to the changing room. I came out wearing it and it ended just above my knees, just the way I liked it, Aubrey saw me and said "That is looking awesome, Ji Eun, you have a killer figure girl" I saw myself in the mirror and the dress was indeed looking good on me. I sent her a hesitant glance through the mirror and she just cocked an eyebrow. I took a deep breath and said "doyouthinkjugHyuniewilllikeit" she smirked teasingly and asked "Can you repeat? I didn't get it." I sighed "do you think Ji Hyun will like it?" She gave a devilish smile and said "Ha... I knew it." I felt myself go beet red and strode towards another set of clothes.

We bought a lot of stuff and back in the car we put them in the trunk and drove away. Ji Hyun was behind the wheel while I in the passenger and Aubrey at the back. I and Aubrey were talking about our past relationships when Ji Hyun gave a fake cough which made me cut my eyes towards him he kept his eyes straight ahead, hands at two and ten on the wheel. "You have a problem with me being in a relationship JH?" I asked "Not at all" he replied still eyes on the road. "Well that little cough looked like it, like excuse me? Sounded to me like a judgmental kind of cough" I said. "Bet you want a sample of the goods, don't you? A little test run? Right here, right now?" I leaned closer to his ear. "You want some Hyunie?"

"My name is Ji Hyun. And no. Not while I'm driving a half-million-dollar automobile." He didn't flinch and didn't look at me. "Ask me later, though, and I might have a different answer." Well that was not an answer I was expecting. It took me by surprise until I heard Aubrey laughing so hard that she had tears in her eyes. "Not gonna lie but that was smooth as hell." She said and I shot her a death glare.

We dropped Aubrey off at her house. She hugged me "Don't be a stranger" she said and bid me goodbye. I sat back in the car and the whole ride back was filled with awkward silence.

CHAPTER 3

JI EUN POV:

After picking up my brother and his girlfriend from the company we headed towards the airfield from where we had to take the plane to reach the island. In order to lose any tracks of where we went we take different vehicles to reach a certain place in order to lose any enemies following us. The whole ride to the airfield was filled with silence.

After sitting in the plane I was damn sure that I am going to go nuts being bored so I went up to Ji Hyun and sat beside him while he was preparing for takeoff (yeah, he knows how to fly planes and most of helicopters). He shot me a questioning glance to which I said "I don't want to get bored the whole flight back so...." I trailed off. He just nodded his head and got back to his work. "Do you want to know how these things work?" he asked me. I was hesitating a bit but then straightened my posture and said "Why not?" he started explaining the work of different buttons and gears while I watched with fascination at his face and his fingers pointing to different things. I had on the headphones with the mic, and I was flipping switches as Ji Hyun pointed them out, checking them against the clipboard balanced on my thigh. We were close together, shoulders brushing, Ji Hyun's right arm propped on my seat back. Once, as I shifted to reach a switch, he caught the clipboard before it fell, and his fingers brushed my thigh when he rebalanced it on my leg.

We landed with a bounce at the island as I was the one helping in landing and I was so excited about it. "Are you sure this is your first time flying something like this?" Ji Hyun asked while removing his headset. I gave him a 'duh' look to which he just chuckled. While descending the plane Ji Wook asked JH "Rough landing?" Ji Hyun just shrugged and said "Your sister helped a lot in it." The look on my brother's face was priceless as he looked at me and blinked a few times.

"I flew a plane" my excitement was through the roof.

I am sure that I am also going to spend my every other flight beside Ji Hyun as he explains different things to me about the switches and buttons.

We entered the house and freshened up by the time dinner was ready. A small bonfire was set up out on the beach with dinner and we sat around the fire munching on our food until I saw a figure moving back in the woods, my blood froze for a moment until the shadow soon took a shape and I saw its face and recognized it as one of the security men and let out a deep sigh. I wondered how they just blend in the shadows and we never know they are there. He came up behind Ji Hyun and whispered something in his ears. He stood up and was going somewhere until Ji Wook asked "What happened?" "Someone came in contact with the movement sensors in the water, it can be some common bleachers who wandered off to here but I am still checking to be on the safer side. Finish the dinner as soon as possible and go inside the house to sleep. I am just going to check with the cameras and sensors." Ji Hyun said and took off towards what I assumed is the control room. I asked my brother to explain it to me and he told me "we have movement sensors all over the island and in the water as well around the island. If someone activates it we get to know that someone came in contact with it. As for the current situation it might be some wild animal roaming in the Jung le or some common bleachers who lost their way in the waters and activated the sensor. Ji Hyun and his men will just check and figure out the nature of the activation and act accordingly." "What do you mean by 'act accordingly'?" I asked. "If it's an animal they will just let it be, if they are some common bleachers they will send them on their right way and help them or if they are activated by some enemies they will finish them off so no need to worry." He explained.

Before entering the house the security checked the whole house and then let us in and after reaching each of our rooms the security again checked each room before letting us in and instructing us to keep it locked unless you recognize the voice calling as one of the security staff. They escorted firstly me off to my room and then my brother. I did my night routine, changed into a comfortable outfit and went to sleep and soon I slipped into a deep slumber of the dreamland.

CHAPTER TWO

Chapter 4-6

Chapter 4

JI WOOK POV:

Four short, sharp raps on the door jolted me awake. I glanced out the window and saw that it was probably an hour or two before dawn, the sky still black but with muted shades of gray staining the horizon where it met the rippling, glinting sea.

"Mr. Wang." It was one of our security men. "Your presence is required, sir. Immediately as possible, please."

I scrambled out of my bed and jumped into my shorts not bothering with shirt or shoes. I saw my girlfriend getting up and pull up a light sundress over her body and follow me out of the room.

Stepping out of the room I realized something significant has happened seeing all of our security men on high alert and with their fingers on the trigger on whatever weapon they were holding and loaded with other weapons too. Something bad has happened.

The security jerked his head toward the dense forest, and set off toward it at a quick walk. He had his rifle tucked into his shoulder, held at the ready, moving in a crouch and sweeping the barrel from side to side. There was no clear path that I could see, but nonetheless he led us unerringly between the trees through near complete darkness to a long, low building. He held open a thick steel door and ushered us in.

This was the security room of this entire island with each TV displaying different cameras fixated on the island and connected the sensors as well. The building was well hidden in the deep forest and was surrounded by a good twenty yards of clearing. The building was windowless, lit only by fluorescent tubes. One wall was entirely taken up by the bank of monitors showing different cameras while opposite it was a floor-to-ceiling case containing an arsenal: assault rifles, as well as a huge assortment of handguns, shotguns, sniper rifles, machetes, flash-bangs and actual grenades, body armor, night vision goggles, and even something huge and terrifying that I thought might be a grenade launcher.

Ji Hyun was sitting at a metal table, a map spread out in front of him, a red pen in one hand and a ruler in the other, marking lines and Xs on the map. He was dressed like the rest of his security force: gray BDUs, black body armor, black "A1S" ball cap, sidearm, knife, and a rifle hanging by its strap from the corner of his chair. He had extra magazines on his body armor webbing, as well.

Ji Hyun didn't have a security team; he had a small mercenary army, each man armed to teeth. So what had them on high alert?

I was about to speak when another security an entered the room and stood beside the door with his palms over each other in front. I looked back at JH. He marked one more X on his map and then swiveled on his chair. "All right, now that we're all here--"

"Wait" I protested "We're not all here. Where's Ji Eun?"

JH's expression hardened, fury darkening his face. "That's why we're here. I'm not going to mince words, sir: Roth took her. Snatched her right out from under my fucking nose"

I was out of my mind. My baby sister was kidnapped by my enemy and I can't do anything except for searching for her. "How the fuck is that possible?" I snarled. "I thought you had this place more secure than any other place?"

"I did. They set off a kind of bomb which fried our circuits and they hit our men on the beach as a distraction. Our men took heavy fire. While that was going on four men infiltrated Ji Eun's room and took her. One man gave pursuit and took down two of them, but got shot in the throat in the process. Not sure he'll make it. It was a quick, precise, and coordinated, and done by serious professionals." JH explained. "Roth's guys lost six men and two were injured." He continued further.

"What about --- what about Ji Eun?" My voice cracked as I said her name.

"Before losing consciousness the man who was on pursuit was able to communicate that she was unhurt." JH clarified. I thanked the stars a little but still my baby sister was in danger which I can't handle.

Mia interrupted our conversation "Wait so you mean some people are killed and some are still after us?"

I was a little pissed at her as I was so worried for Ji Eun at that time "Mia, baby. Do me a favor, okay? Shut the hell up." I snapped at her. This shut her up but not before giving me a sad pout.

I crossed the room to stand in front of JH. I had two inches on him, and used them to good effect, staring down at him with anger in my eyes. "Swear to me right now that this couldn't have been prevented, Ji Hyun."

He stared back, chin lifting. "It was a calculated strike, Mr. Wang. It was fucking surgical. The whole thing with Ji Eun took less than three minutes from first contact. There was nothing else we could have done, sir. I've got two wounded and one dead or...as good as dead."

"What are we doing to get her back?" I asked stepping back.

"I will rip this planet open to find her," Ji Hyun said. "I swear on my immortal soul I will find her, and I will end the life of every motherfucker involved in taking her." The vicious look in JH's eyes told me he meant it.

I felt Mia shiver a little beside me and saw her looking at Ji Hyun feared by the rage in his eyes. I put my hand around her shoulder to give her some comfort.

Ji Hyun turned towards one of his men and told him to stay by our side 24/7. "Guys, I am sorry but privacy is going out the window until this is over. He will stay beside you at all times, even in your rooms." He said pointing at the one who brought us here.

"Are you going after her alone?" I asked.

"Hell no, I am taking one of my alpha members with me along with some other security men but I've increased the security around the island and on each of you." he stated and then made some other instructions on his mic and gave me a reassuring nod before we headed out of the building back to our rooms.

Stay safe baby sis, Ji Hyun is coming for you. I said a little prayer and went back.

CHAPTER5

JI EUN POV:

I've seen some pretty shit in my life, but that scene? I'll have nightmares for the rest of my life, that's for damn sure. One second I was sleeping and having a nice little dream about Ji Hyun--although I'd deny that if pressed-- and then the door was exploding and four dark shapes surrounded me. They tossed a black bag over my head, jerked my arms behind my back and wrapped zip-ties tight around my wrists, and shoved me forward.

As soon as I got to my senses I started thrashing and kicking, biting at whatever flesh was closest to me.

"LET ME GO YOU FUCKING FUCKS!" I screamed. I felt my foot connect with bone, and I kicked again, as hard as I could. I heard a grunt and a curse. "I'll kick all of your fucking asses. Put me the fuck down!"

I felt a press of cold metal against my temple and a gruff voice saying "shut the fuck up" with a Brazilian accent. That shut me up. I heard guns being fired everywhere around me and one was shot so near me, the man holding me fell to the ground, I tried running away but two pair of hands grabbed my both hands and dragged me back.

They carried me and put me on a boat, cold, hard, wet rubber under my legs. Again a gun was pressed under my skull to keep me shut. I heard them talking in a different language. Italian? Brazilian? I don't have any idea. But from there tone I could guess that they were talking about me.

The boat was sailing along the waves and occasionally the boat swayed in different directions pushing me from side to side because I don't have anything to get hold of as my hands are tied. A relatively bigger wave came and that left me drenched from head to toe and as a result my upper torso was on full display for the goons because who wears a bra while sleeping? The cold breeze made me shiver and I could hear my kidnappers talking and touching me everywhere.

I was disgusted by them touching me but I had to stay put because any type of resistance can end up in me being dead. So I stayed put.

After some distance I was hauled into another boat, this one was faster than the former one. I got that we were going to change a number of vehicles to lose traces. We changed two vehicles till now. This boat was bigger than the previous one so I had more space to scoot farther from the men but they were still murmuring something.

After I don't know how much time the boat stopped and a gruff voice said near my ear "I am freeing you, make any move to escape and you die. Understood?" I nodded my head. "I want words, bitch." He said with anger. "Yes, understood" I replied. He cut the zip-ties around my wrists and pulls the black bag over my head, it was still dark but dawn was not far. He motioned me to move up the rope ladder connecting to a small ship.

With some difficulty but I went up the ladder and landed safely on the ship. Upon reaching I saw many men there with a shit load of weapons in their hands and different boxes placed across the floor. All of their eyes were on me and I seriously hoped to have something to cover me up but I had nothing so I just ignored them.

On the ship I was locked up in a small room. I was given food there and I dug in immediately as I was famished, and I needed to pee. After about 15 minutes of banging on the door it opened and he asked "WHAT DO YOU WANT?" "I need to pee" I said. "Then pee here only" he replied annoyed. "I can't. Please. There must be a toilet on this ship?" I said. He rolled his eyes and made me follow him to what I expected to be a toilet. He stopped in front of a door and told me to go inside. He kept the door open and looked at me. "At least close the door or turns around" I said "Just do it" he replied. "I suggest you take a book because this one is going to be long one---"He cut me off with closing the door with a loud bang.

A wave of relief washed over me as I peed and I looked for something or anything present there. I saw a pen lying on the floor under the wash basin. I picked it up and washed it. I thought for some time as to hide it where? As I don't have any pockets or anything. A very stupid idea popped in my head but I had no other option. I stuck that open up in my vagina. It felt weird there but I adjusted after some seconds. I washed my hands and that's when the guy opened the door glaring at me. After I was done he took me back to my cell and all the way back I was walking funny and I hoped he did not notice it.

Once I was back in my cell my first instinct was to take it out, but then I got to thinking. I knew I was gonna need it at some point, but not when that would be. Probably not on the boat--that would be a waste. I'd probably need it when we got where we were going, wherever that was. So in it stayed.

I was going bat shit crazy as I was overthinking. It had been two days I was locked up in this room—according to number of times I've been given food. And never had I forgotten about the pen up in my pussy.

After almost I don't know how many days we got off the boat and went to an airfield. We took a plane from there. I asked the man who was with me "where are we going?" "Brazil" he replied clearly annoyed. I scrunched up my face and buckled in for takeoff.

After about four to five hours we landed and I was kind of relived to set my foot on and rather than seeing sea all around myself. I recalled all the events from my kidnapping and remembered that we have changed 5 vehicles including the car that we were in.

The car stopped in front of a building and I was escorted out of it and in the lift. The man with me punched a code in the elevator and it moved upwards. It stopped at 43rd floor. We stepped out of it and I saw a man in a fine suit standing with his back towards us, as if waiting for us. My kidnapper shoved me forward and went back down in the elevator. As if on cue the suited man turned and said "Welcome Miss Wang Ji Eun." Right in front of me in flesh and blood was standing Roth.

CHAPTER 6

JI EUN POV:

I was not scared. *No.* I was petrified. I can see the rage in his eyes and the hatred but I was not going to show him the week side of me. I was standing straight and bold before him.

"I like your act of showing that you are not scared of me but I know you are indeed scared so no need to hide it." He said coldly. *Shit.* I took a deep breath before replying "bold of you to assume that I would be scared of you. Don't forget that my brother is a mafia too and so was my father." I crossed my arms over my chest and gave him a scoff. I swear I saw a hint of amusement in his eyes by my remark. *Yes.*

He called someone on the phone and said "Yuri, come upstairs."After a few minutes the man who brought me here who I assume is named Yuri came and eyed me a bit as if asking if I said anything? I just shrugged my shoulders. Roth said "I've been informed that she was kept in a small room which was not more than a cell while she was brought here? Is that true?" he asked. Yuri nodded. "Why she was not provided a better room as I've specifically mentioned that she was bait?" he said rather calmly. *What? I am bait?*

Before Yuri could answer Roth pulled out a pocket knife from his right pocket and stabbed him in the ribs. The movement was so fast that one can't even see it coming and it is done. By the time you realize what has happened you will be on the ground dying. After some seconds Yuri died. Some men came from the other room and cleaned up the place and took the body.

"So Miss Wang as you must have figured out that you are bait to catch your brother so you will not die so soon. Maybe when I kill your brother and that bodyguard's of his, Ji Hyun." Roth said turning toward me. "Would you like to take a shower?" he asked. I nodded as I desperately needed a shower at that time. I don't know how long I have travelled and how many days have gone by.

My only one mantra was. Ji Hyun is coming. Ji Hyun is coming. Ji Hyun is coming. Ji Hyun is coming.

I went to take a shower and Roth shamelessly followed me inside. I motioned him to go outside but he denied and stood by the sink watching me. He made it clear that if want to shower I have to do it in front of him or nothing. I tried to ignore his presence and stripped off my clothes and started to shower. I cleaned myself thoroughly and even down there fully aware of the weapon I hid there. Then I shampooed my hair and washed them. As I turned off the shower and turned towards the towel rack I saw Roth watching me intently which made my skin crawl and I wished I could shower all over again or at least claw his eyes out. I dried myself and surprisingly was provided new clothes with even decent undergarments.

The next few days went by me doing exercise all day as I had nothing to do otherwise and him doing his business, watching me and sometimes join me in exercise. I learned a few things about him. His right hand man Mike was also his childhood best friend who handles all of his illegal businesses. He had a smooth way of killing people with just a pocket knife. So fast that no one can see it coming.

He had killed almost 7 people in my presence and that was the same pattern of him killing. I was no longer fazed by his method of killing as now I have seen how he moves with the knife so I can predict when it happens. Thanks to my one of my ex who was an MMA fighter who taught me these kinds of things and gave me lessons of self-defense. His men dare not come to him empty handed or they will get no less than death. He was always calm while doing every work and never even raised his voice. This made him all the more dangerous

I was never allowed to go out of the room and Roth was always in the room with me watching me intently. I had to shower in his presence only. Still I managed to survive through this by my constant mantra that Ji Hyun is coming to save me.

I thought of sometimes taking out he pen from down there but Roth was constantly watching my every move and I don't want to take that risk. I would choose a vaginal infection any day over being dead. *Duh.*

Then one day finally came that Roth had to go out of the country for some work and I was finally alone but still stuck in the room. The elevator had an opening in the room only but it can only open through a key or a passcode and I knew neither of them. After some time the door of the elevator opened and I saw Mike come through it covered all in blood and stumbling a little. He had devilish smirk on his face. He came towards me as I backed off far into the wall and had no escape now. He tried to grasp my wrist but I jerked it free. I smelled alcohol on him. He was drunk.

"Roth has such an eye candy by his side for so many days. Finally he is out of country so I can have you all to myself." Mike slurred. "I don't think it is a good idea." I said. "He will probably kill you for harming me." I continued. "He will not kill me. I am his childhood best friend. Do you think he will harm me for raping a hostage? No way in hell." He clarified.

Saying this he charged towards me and I dodged him successfully and ran towards the other side of the room, my defense kicking in and adrenaline rushing through my veins. "Just give up already." He shouted at me. 'Not without a fight' I told myself.

You want to rape me? Not without putting up a fight fucker and a good one at that. Fight me.

CHAPTER THREE

Chapter 7-9

CHAPTER 7

Thanks to the MMA fighter of my past boyfriend who taught me some tricks of self-defense and even Brazilian jujitsu, I can defend myself and even try to escape. I mentally laughed at the irony that I am going to use Brazilian jujitsu in Brazil. So let's break some shit.

I took out the pen and stuck it in between my teeth-- yuck--and grabbed his palm with both hands, then twisted until it wouldn't twist anymore, hooking my leg around his arm so the back of my knee braced the cap of his elbow. Grinning up into his surprised face, I then pulled back with both hands while rocking my body in the opposite direction. *Snap.* His elbow now bent in two directions.

The entire move took less than three seconds. I took the pen in my fist, spat into his face. Steeled myself, jaw clenched, squeamishness locked down tight. He saw it coming. I made sure he did. I held the pen up high, palm of one hand cupping the back of my pen-wielding fist, slammed it down as hard as I could into his eye socket, putting all my weight, all my strength into the move. It pierced his eye like...well, like an ink pen through Jell-O. I hit resistance, and the pen stuck. He was thrashing, gurgling, twitching. I smelled shit. I put my palm to the end of the pen where it protruded from his skull, slammed my fist down onto the back of my hand like a hammer, driving the pen deeper into his brain.

He went still. I checked his breathing and his pulse to be sure. He was dead. I killed a man. I felt bile rise in my throat, I rushed to the bathroom and puked my guts out. I washed my face and mouth and came back in the room and started searching him. I unlaced his boots and wore them; I don't want to run through Brazil barefoot, tying the laces as tight as I can so they don't fall off my feet. I took a key from his pocket and hoped for it to be the key to the elevator. I also found a folding knife in his pocket and took it. I tried the key into the elevator and it opened. *Thank the lord.*

As the elevator closed I pushed the button marked as P as I hoped it meant parking and the elevator descended down and opened in a dark place which I assumed is the parking lot. There were a group of boys there eying me, assessing me up and down. They had a car and I need that car. I took out the pocket knife and pointed it towards one of them. They held up their hands in defense and shook their heads. I pointed towards the car and one of them took out a pair of keys from his pocket and threw it towards me. I took them and slipped them in one of my fingers. I started going towards the car still pointing the knife at them. One of them came forward and I tightened my hold around the knife and held it high. He said "No harm, take the money." pointing towards the car. I assumed it is his car. He opened the trunk of the car and handed me some money after taking some for his own. I nodded at him showing my gratitude and he nodded back saying "boss is no good" pointing at the building above and I said "yes" not caring if he understood or not.

I sat in the car and started it pulling out of the parking space and sped towards the nearest road I saw. After about 30 minutes of driving I was drenched in my sweat and probably on a highway.

Brazil is fucking hot. I still had that mantra that Ji Hyun is coming, Ji Hyun is coming, Ji Hyun is coming.

I stopped at a gas station and filled some gas in the car and went into the shop nearby. I bought some snacks from there and a prepaid phone. The shopkeeper eyed me seeing me all in sweat and asked "American?" "Yes" I answered. He gave me a sim of local number and said "just put the pin code mentioned on the sim before the number and you can make the call." I nodded my head and said a 'thank you' not sure whether he understood or not. I also bought map from there to know where I am heading.

I hopped into the car and drove off. I stopped somewhere in the middle and got out of the car. I opened the trunk of the car and took out a pair of shorts and a shirt from there. I got back in the driver's seat and opened the dashboard and found a bill of 5 of whatever currency used there. *Shit*. Now I don't have any money either.

I took out the phone and followed the instructions to make a call and dialed my brother's number from memory.

The line rang once, twice, three times...four, five, and six. "Come on, bro," I muttered, "pick up the damn phone."

I heard a click, and then a smooth male voice. "Who is this?"

I choked, blinked back blurry stinging salt out of my eyes. The relief I felt was immeasurable. NOPENOPENOPE. I'm not crying. For sure I'm not crying. "I—Ji Hyun? It's—it's Ji

Eun."

A pause. "Ji Eun?" Another pause. "Sit-rep? Um I mean what is your situation?"

"I know what a fucking sit-rep means. I watch TV. I am fine. I got away." Ji Hyun sighed on the other end of the phone and asked "How did you escape?" I didn't want to recall that part so I just said I got away somehow.

"Where are you?" he asked. "Brazil. Heading out of Sao Paulo toward--well, I don't know how to pronounce it. A city on the coast, south of Sao Paulo. Starts with a 'G' and has an 'A' with a slant over it at the end. Gwar-yooh-jah or some shit." I answered. "Guaruja." He said it gwar-ooh-zha. "Good plan. I can be there in--less than twelve hours. Are you hurt?" I hesitated. "I'm fine. I can last twelve hours."

"Ji Eun" he said my name....softly. Strangely inflected, like with emotion. It made my heart squirm and stomach flop. "What did they do to you?" he further asked. "Nothing, really. Nothing to worry about. I got away. I am alive, not permanently damaged and, I am in transit."

"How did you manage that?" "I stole a dude's car and stopped at a gas station, bought a prepaid phone and a map. I've got my route mapped out. I don't know if I have enough fuel to go till there but I can walk if needed." I said. "I'm impressed" he sounded like he wanted to say a lot more but kept it to himself. "Do you think you're being pursued?" he asked. I checked the rear view mirror and saw nothing unusual besides the cars on the highway. "No. I don't think so" I answered. "I am sure when Roth finds out what I had done to run away he will send out groups of men after me." I said further. "You met Roth?" he asked amused. "Y-Yes" my voice broke and I was on the verge of tears. *No. not gonna cry.* "Yea, I met Roth and he is a vicious son of a bitch."

"What did you have to do to get away?" this, said softly in that same concerned tone. "Nothing I am willing to talk about on phone. I gotta keep my shit together. Maybe after you've rescued me I'll let myself think about it a little bit, but for now I'm fine. Just get here as soon as possible Ji Hyun." I said not wavering a bit.

"Get to Guaruja, Ji Eun. Find a hide-out, don't talk to anyone and don't stop for anything. I'll be there as soon as I possibly can. You are going to be fine. I am on my way." He said. Tears were pressing the back of my eyes and threatened to fall out. "Yes Ji Hyun, I am fine. This is like a road trip, just in..... Brazil." I said trying to convince myself more than anything.

"Just get here." I said and ended the call before he can hear the knot in my throat. I didn't cry. I was just sweating...from my tear ducts. I had a little sniffle.

No big deal.

Ji Hyun is coming. Ji Hyun is coming. Ji Hyun is coming.

CHAPTER 8

JI EUN POV:

After ending the call I wore the clothes I took from the car's trunk to disguise myself a little bit. I started the car and drove off in the direction shown on the map for Guaruja. There was mild traffic on the road, cars moving at a constant pace, tourist roaming around the area clicking pictures and giggling. After some kilometers of driving the engine of the car coughed, sputtered and gave out.

I tried starting the car again but to no avail. I got out the car shoving the bill of 5 and the pre-paid phone in the shorts pocket, took the map and folded it after looking at the rout to take and started walking in the direction, at least I was not walking barefoot. The people there shot me a questioning glance but soon retreated to their own matters. After walking for half hour the rout showed a mountain I had no choice but to climb that mountain and that's what I did. I was drenched in sweat but was not giving up that fast.

Brazil is fucking hot.

After crossing two mountains I saw a little café on the side. Without thinking any further I entered it. The bell on the door chimed announcing my arrival. There was an old lady at the desk and the café had no customers. I approached the desk and the old lady gave me a smile. I hesitantly took out the crumpled 5 bill from my pocket and put it on the table, flattening it with my hands and outturned my pockets to show that it is all I have. I made a gesture of food with my hands and said "Eat?" The lady gave me a reassuring smile and vanished behind the doors and came back with a glass of water filled with ice and gave it to me. I gulped the water and never have I been so satisfied with a gulp of water. I chugged down the water and realized how thirsty I was. The lady again vanished behind the doors after motioning towards me to take a seat.

After some minutes the lady came towards me with a tray full of food. I don't know how much the 5 bill valued but I was dead sure it was not worth this much food. I stood up and showed the lady my pockets again to indicate that I don't have any more money. She patted my shoulder and made me sit and indicated me to eat the food. I looked at the tray of food in front of me and my stomach growled at the sight of that. The lady let out a chuckle and took her position back behind the desk.

In no time I finished the food as I was famished and finally there was some food in my stomach. I made my way to the desk but there was no sign of the old lady. Just then she emerged from the back door with a pillow and a blanket and gave them to me. She led me through the back door towards a single bed and looked at me and said "Sleep here?" tears welled up in my eyes and soon started flowing down. The old lady's expression changed to that of a worried one as to why was I crying. She again asked "no sleep?" I shook my head and wiped my tears and hugged her so tight. She patted my back to calm me down and helped me to bed. As she was going I held her hand and gave her a smile and said "Thank you" she placed her other hand over mine holding her and said "We say obrigado" I nodded my head in understanding and said again "obrigado" his old lady who doesn't even know me did so much for me and this showed that humanity still existed in this cruel world.

She came back with some clean clothes and offered them to me. I accepted them and she also motioned me to the bathroom to take a shower. As I entered the bathroom, one look at me and anyone could tell that I desperately needed a shower. I was covered in dirt from head to toe and all my clothes were also soiled from dirt. I felt grateful to this woman for giving me shelter for the night. I took a bit long and warm shower that relaxed my muscles from the excess exertion of the day. I avoided thinking about anything as I would end up thinking about how I killed Mike. How that pen went through his eye. How I snapped his arm in two directions and he shat himself, blood oozing out from where the pen stuck out from his skull. *Shit. Shitshishit.* All those memories flashed before my eyes. I shook my head to get rid of those memories, washed myself and came out I wore my clothes and went to bed. I soon slipped into a deep slumber as I was exhausted from the day.

I saw me and Ji Hyun holding hands and running on a beach with wide smiles on our faces, my hair blowing around in the wind and soon I was taken over by darkness again.

CHAPTER 9

My eyes snapped open at the sound of a door being slammed shut. I opened my eyes and blinked to adjust to the light coming through the window beside me. I was disorientated as to where I was then everything came back as a lighting flash to me that I was not on a vacation but rather on a run for my life. Every hair on my body stood to attention and was on full alert mode. I ducked under the window and tried to locate the position from where the sound came. I popped my head till my eyes to see outside and saw two black SUV's were parked. *Shit. They found me.* But how? I left no traces as long as I remember and was definitely not followed by someone.

Now was not the time to think about that. Now was the time to think on how to escape. A shrill scream broke me out of my thoughts and I recognized it as the old lady's. I was feeling very bad at the thought of the old lady getting hurt because of me. I gave no thought to it and dashed towards the door of the café and made my out of it.

I opened the driver's side door of an SUV and hoped in. I started the car and put it in reverse gear and made my way out of the driveway and onto the main road. I saw in the rear view mirror more men getting in the car behind me and following me at full speed. They were constantly shooting at me. A loud bang and the back mirror shed to pieces. I dug out the phone from my pocket and dialed Ji

Hyun's number. He picked it up at the second ring and answered "Hello?" he smooth voice came through the phone. Tears pricked my eyes at his voice but I pushed them back and focused on driving.

"Ji Hyun they found me and they are following me" I answered. "How" I heard fear in his voice. "I don't know. I am sure I left no traces behind and also the car broke down so I had to walk almost two miles on mountain road and I stopped at a small café on the mountain and the lady there allowed me to spend the night there and in the morning there were two black cars outside it. I don't have any idea how they found me." I answered back. "Do you have any weapon with you?" he asked. "I only have this phone and yeah I have a knife with me." I answered. "Wait a second" saying this I tossed the phone on the passenger seat and turned the steering wheel to the right and slammed on the brakes this gave me a moment to speed off in the dust that formed from the brakes. I again resumed the call on the phone. "Sorry to leave you hanging. What were you saying?" I asked. "Where are you?" he asked. "I don't know exactly but the café was 2 kilometers from Guaruja and the road I am currently at has barren land on both sides." I informed. "Ok Ji Eun, listen to me carefully. Step on the gas and keep going in that direction after about half a kilometer there will be a forest on one side. Abandon the car on roadside and run into the woods and try to hide if possible or just run through the woods. I will be there in about 15 minutes. Understood?" he asked. "Yes understood" I said. I heard a click and the call ended.

I tossed the phone on the passenger seat and floored the gas pedal and the car shot forward. I checked the rear view mirror and now there were two black cars behind me closing in on me. "Shit" I muttered. After 5 minutes of driving I saw trees on the right side of the road. I increased the speed and the black cars were closing in on me. When the woods became dense enough I slammed on the breaks which caused my pursuers to shot past me. I jumped out of the car with the phone clutched tightly in my hand and ran into the woods. I called Ji Hyun. He picked it up at the first ring. "Ji Hyun I am into the woods but they are still behind me and they are faster than me." I said. "Just keep running forward I am almost there." He replied. The men had machine guns and they were constantly firing bullets at me. They were ordered to bring me dead or alive, and they will not return empty-handed.

After a couple of minutes I saw a road and a car there and then I saw Ji Hyun. A wave of relief gushed through me. I ran at my full speed towards his car. He saw me coming, got out of the car and shot my pursuers. He opened the passenger seat and I sat in the car and we drove off from there. There were now more cars following us constantly firing from time to time. Ji Hyun was firing in return. The back glass of the car broke to pieces and I hid my head with my hands.

Ji Hyun tossed a gun in my lap I took it, composed myself and held it in both hands and started firing at the cars behind us while alternatively hiding behind the seat. Ji Hyun grinned at me and I asked "what are you smiling at?" these seats doesn't really block the bullets, you know?" he replied showing me the holes in the seat and then the bullets shot in the dashboard of the car. I took several deep breaths and started firing again. As a car was closing in on me I took aim and shot at the driver and the bullet went in his throat and that car swiveled at the side, crashed into the divider and turned upside down.

Ji Hyun looked at it in the side view mirror and said "bull's eye" while grinning from ear to ear. "Okay, now I am going to slow down and I want you to duck down when they come beside me." he said. "I am not ducking down anywhere I can also shoot and that was a live example you just had there." I said with a little anger.

"Okay, so brace yourself so that you don't bang your head against the window." He said. That left me shocked as what is he going to do? He slowed down right away and our pursuers soon came beside us and they were constantly shooting at us. As a reflex I ducked down to avoid getting shot. Ji Hyun cut the steering wheel to the left and our car banged with the one beside us. That sent them off guard and they stopped shooting, we took advantage of it and Ji Hyun again slammed into their car and I fired at the driver and the car went off road and turned upside down.

When I turned to look at Ji Hyun he had a smirk plastered on his face. I shot him a questioning look and he said "I told you to duck down but you didn't listen. So if you don't want to get killed just do as you're told." My anger boiled and I burst out saying "I stabbed a guy in the eyeball with a pen I'd kept hidden in my cunt for over a week. I shoved it so far into his fucking brain that he died instantly. And that was after I broke his arm like a twig. I did this because he was in the process of raping me. I put on his smelly boots--- and I stole a car, stopped for supplies, drove to fucking Guaruja, and walked several miles in the blazing heat, most of that distance either in the sand or uphill, without having any food or water. And then I stole a car right out from underneath the very men who were hunting me." I was getting a little worked up at this point. "And then--and then!--then I was nearly shot several times just now by those assholes back there. So I think at this point, JH, there isn't much that's going to faze me. Figure out how you want to ambush these fuckers, and I'll help you kill every single goddamn one of those pussies."

This outburst earned me a mixture of several expressions from hurt to anger to amusement all the way. He shot me a sympathetic glance and trained his eyes on the road again. I scoffed a little and looked away crossing my arms on my chest.

Ji Hyun put his hand on my shoulder and patted it in a way to comfort me and said "You did well and it was to save yourself, nothing to regret." This did calm me down and I was glad for it or I would have burst out crying and I don't want to cry now.

CHAPTER FOUR

Chapter 10-12

CHAPTER 10

After several minutes of silence he asked "are they still following us? Look several cars back." I turned around and they were still behind us about half a mile back. "Yes, they are" I replied. "Roth's men don't give up. They keep coming until we kill them or they catch us." "No shit. They don't dare go back to Roth without results to show him" I said. Ji Hyun glanced at me, his gaze sharp, and his voice soft. "No?"

I shook my head as I returned to my seat and buckled up. "No. They don't dare. He doesn't accept failure or excuses. You do what he tells you to do, or you die trying. If you show up and you haven't carried out his orders to the letter, he'll kill you. And you'll never even see it coming." "How does he kill them?" he asked.

I blinked hard. "Knife to the ribs" I tapped two fingers over my heart. "He's got this switchblade, keeps it in his pocket. He'll just be talking, calm as anything. One second he's smiling, hands in his pockets, casual, the picture of understanding and congeniality. The next? That blade is between their ribs, and they're dead. He does it so fast, so easily. Doesn't even blink. I saw him do it at least six times in the four days I was his prisoner. He must pay those guys really well if they're willing to risk death any time they're in the room with him."

Changing the topic at hand he said "So now I just have to loose these men" "Do what you'd do if you were alone. Don't worry about me." I said. With this he turns the car in a left lane and the black cars behind us followed suit, but still quite far from us. He then turned the car into a narrow gravel road running parallel to the highway. He turned into a driveway and stopped the car. He rounded it and pulled out a black duffel bag out of the trunk and put it around his shoulder. The bag made a loud clanking sound as he did that.

We entered a backyard with long grasses and Ji Hyun put the bag at his feet and opened it after wiping off some sweat from his brow. As he opened the bag my mouth was hanging open at the stuff inside it. The bag was full of assault rifles, machine guns, handguns, pistols and other type of guns I didn't know the names of.

He took out two handguns and put them in the vest he was wearing. Then he hauled an assault rifle on his shoulder and handed me one gun as well. He then took out four spare clips and handed them to me. "You can reload those, right?" he asked.

I showed him I could by ejecting the clip, checking it, and sliding it back in place, tapping it home with the hell of my palm--gently, contrary to popular silver-screen mythology. "Where do you want me?"

There were some drums scattered around the grass and he motioned me to hide behind one of them lying on my stomach. I got into my position and glanced up at Ji Hyun. "Well? Don't just stand there, doofus. Go find your own spot."

He shook his head at me, a smirk quirking the corner of his mouth. When he was gone I closed my eyes and let myself feel the fear. I was fucking terrified, to put it frankly. None of this was normal, even for me. I'd been through some shit in my life, but lying in wait, preparing to ambush men who were trying to kill me? It was new. And not fun.

I do not recommend it.

I was on my belly, pointing the gun through the gap between the barrels I was hiding behind. Soon enough a man came through the fence looking here and there to spot us but he couldn't. Another man came behind him. They both had what will be a compact form of a machine gun. I was just aiming my gun ready to shoot whenever needed. I didn't want to shoot too fast and ruin the ambush JH has set.

I will only shoot after Ji Hyun has started.

As if on cue three more men emerged behind the two before and a loud bang resonated from the walls and the fifth man fell to the ground. It all happened in a blink of an eye. Another BANG!! And the first man in the line fell to the ground. The remaining three went in three different directions. Taking my cue I aimed the gun on the third man's torso and pulled the trigger. The man lurched forward a red spot forming in his stomach. *Shit. I have to shoot him again.* I aimed again for his forehead this time and shot again. This time the man fell down but the bullet didn't go through his head but through his throat. The remaining two started firing randomly in all directions.

One round of bullets was shot near me and made me scream. One man spotted me and came near me with an evil grin on his face. As soon as he approached me another round of bullets came and the man in front of me fell to the ground and the bullets have totally embedded in his face. *Gross.* I felt bile rise in my throat and I puked all the nastiness out of my mouth. Ji Hyun came near the last man and pointed at his gun. He dropped it to the ground and lift up his hands in surrender. Ji Hyun asked him something to which he answered while his hands still above his head. Ji Hyun pointed his gun at his head and shot. He fell to the ground. Ji Hyun came towards me and helped me stand up.

"Okay?" Ji Hyun asked me. I shook my head and said "I'm fine." Ji Hyun barked a laugh and said "Well that was clear as mud. I'll ask again, Ji Eun. you good?" I closed my eyes and focused on breathing evenly. "Just get me out of here. Please?" Ji Hyun held my face in his hands and said "Look at me Ji Eun, you did great. They're gone. We're safe now." "I shot him twice." I retorted. "That is because he was going to kill you." He soothed me. "There's nothing wrong in that." He further said.

He helped me keep my balance and checked the pockets of each men lying on the ground and took whatever they had, safety clips, money, pocket knife and other things and shoved it into his bag and slung it over his shoulder. The high waist grass was wet and crimson. I avoided looking at the bodies at my feet but the air had a strong stench of blood and sweat. Bile rose in my throat but I kept it down.

"Ji Hyun, does killing someone ever gets easier?" I asked. "It never gets easier, you just get used to it. I almost pissed myself the first time I killed an enemy. That was way before I worked for Mr. Wang." He said not looking at me. "I puked." I said. "Still better than me." he said.

We reached the car; he put the bag in the trunk and got behind the wheel while I sat in the passenger seat. I looked behind me but found no black cars just a few highway cars were there. I heaved a sigh of relief.

We drove off onto the highway.

CHAPTER 11

JI EUN POV:

Five minutes onto the highway the car drive was silent and the sexual tension in the air was very high. I was strangely.... turned on. I was not wearing bra and my nipples were perking up. I tried crossing and uncrossing my hands over my chest but it only worsened the situation as the friction made them stand to attention.

I was aware of my every move, how my thighs rubbed together to ease the tension between my legs. I was also aware of Ji Hyun's every move, his hands on the steering wheel while one hand alternating between the steering wheel and the gear.

I was occasionally glancing at Ji Hyun and caught him stealing glances at me. Well I was not the only one affected by the tension in the air. I have the same effect on him as he has on me. I averted my gaze on his hands again thinking how they will feel on my skin. The hard touch of his hands on the soft skin of my body touching every inch. *Shit. Ji Eun get a hold of yourself and stop thinking like that.*

I was constantly shifting in my seat. My palms were itchy. I wanted to paw his shirt off and run my hands on his abs and over his whole body. God, I wanted him.

I didn't want to want him but in that moment I was frustrated with need. I stole a glance at him and caught him just looking away. He had been staring at my tits. I mean they were very prominent with my arousal.

I cut my eyes to Ji Hyun again and caught him staring at me; he briefly turned his gaze on the road to navigate a turn and then again looked at me. He ever so slowly trailed his eyes down to my tits and then back up and then he turned his gaze on the road again.

He shifted in his seat more like squirmed and I caught sight of his erection throbbing at the zipper of his jeans. He was trying to suppress it and tried to adjust it.

"Don't look at me like that, Ji Eun," he growled. His eyes returned to the road and he gripped the steering wheel with both hands and shifted in the driver's seat. "Then don't you look at me like that either." I turned away and tried to focus on the scenery outside the window. "I'm not looking at you like anything," he said. "And neither am I." My words were given a lie by the way I tried to steal a look at him, and caught him doing the same.

Silence.

"It's just the adrenaline," I said. "Right" His hands were twisting the faded leather of the steering wheel as if trying to choke it into submission. "It'll pass on its own. It doesn't mean anything." I tried chewing on my lip, biting down hard enough to cause pain. Nope. That didn't help either.

We drove in complete silence for a several minutes. Neither of us daring to look at each other, neither of us daring to cross the invisible line drawn between us.

He seemed to know exactly where we were going, and it wasn't back to the epicentre of Sao Paulo. If I had my directions right, we were heading east. I didn't care, though. Or rather, I didn't have the mental capacity to care. I knew I was gonna be safe as long as Ji Hyun is with me.

Right in that moment all I could think was of how needy I was and the only person to quench that thirst was only a foot away from me and I couldn't do anything about it.

Then a spark flew. He took his hand off the wheel and set it at the side of my seat. His hand was ever so slowly crawling towards my body and it made my body sing with need. I tried to avoid it and pretended to see out of the window but I was aware of his every move.

He placed his hand on my knee making me gasp at the skin contact and caressed my knee cap. His touch was surprisingly gentle yet firm. I cut my gaze to him and saw him already looking at me. A simple smile playing on his lips and in that moment I just wanted to kiss him. He again turned his eyes towards the road.

After a couple of moments he broke the silence "We are almost there." I saw that we are no longer on the highway but on a road parallel to it having more turns. "You have a house here? In Brazil?" I asked shocked. "No I don't, but Thresh arranged one for spending the night and made sure it was safe." He replied. "Who is Thresh?" I asked. He chuckled before replying "I might not be able to tell precisely. Why don't you look for yourself? I can just say that a terminator would look a pussy in front of him."

He turned the car into the driveway and there was a one storey house there. Ji Hyun stopped the car and turned off the ignition. He got out of the car and so did I. As we were approaching the car a man of about 7 feet came out from the door and he had to duck and turn a little sideways to get through that little door.

He was Thresh. His body was built like he spent 20 hours a day in the gym. His biceps was as big as my thighs and his hand were so big I can't compare to anything. I can say he can hold my whole head in his one hand. He did make terminator look like a pussy or he was the real life terminator.

I dint notice I was staring at him until Ji Hyun cleared his throat. I broke out of my daze and looked at Ji Hyun. He said "Ji Eun, meet Thresh. Thresh meet Ji Eun, Mr Wang's sister." Thresh took my hand for a handshake and I was scared that my little hand might get crushed but his grip was rather gentle. "Where did you meet this hulk" I blurted out before I could stop my words escaping my mouth. Both Thresh and Ji Hyun burst out laughing. "I have a whole group of alpha one security currently working for Mr Wang, under me. He is just one of them." Ji Hyun simply shrugged.

I didn't know that we have a whole alpha security following us. *Damn fuck.* How can one not see a 7 foot man walking behind oneself? Like it is not easy to hide a body as big as that. But then he is in alpha so it will be one of his specialities. To hide himself and hide well.

"Boss, the sensors are all in place so are the cameras. You can monitor all of them on your phone, I've connected them. I am going to prepare for the things ahead. This place is safe for at least next 50 hours, no more. You can spend the night and take a good rest." Thresh said handing the phone to Ji Hyun and nodding at hm. Ji Hyun nodded back at him and they parted ways.

I was still shocked at the fact that Thresh addressed Ji Hyun as 'Boss' and I can't get over that fact ever.

We were once again alone and as soon as we entered the house the sexual tension in the air rose up to high alert and the fire could be seen in both of our eyes.

CHAPTER 12

JI EUN POV:
SMUT WARNING

We moved into the house. Ji Hyun opened the door and ushered me in and then came in locking the door behind him.

And then, with a growl of irritated acquiescence, he moved so he was pressed up against me, erection hard against my belly, face tipped down, mouth centimeters from mine. "Tell me no," he murmured. I should have. I couldn't. "Ji Eun" It was a demand, a repetition of his injunction to say no. "Ji Hyun" At my use of his name, he seemed to swell and his fingers gathered the skin-tight cotton of my T-shirt into his fists. "Last chance, Ji Eun. Tell me to stop."

I dint want him to stop and moreover I want him. He pinned me on the wall and smashed his lips onto me making me gasp at the sudden action, giving him access to my mouth as a result. He slipped his tongue inside my mouth exploring every corner of my mouth with his tongue and that moment was of pure bliss.

He tapped my thigh and I wrapped them around his waist. He carried me through the house in the bedroom and placed me on the bed not breaking the kiss. We pulled apart from each other to get air. He didn't take off my shirt, he literally ripped it off of me and now I was only in my shorts and panties. I discarded my shorts and he moved his hands to rip my panties but I stopped him. "Don't, it's the only pair I've got." I said. "I've got you clean clothes from your closet. There are in the bag, so don't worry about it." He replied and in a split second I was bare in front of him.

He stood up and removed his shirt over his head and discarded them on the floor. I sat up on the bed and ran my hands from his chest to his abs and down to the 'v' in his pants. I played with the buckle of his belt on his jeans and unbuckled it. I slid his jeans and boxers down and let his manhood free. I gave it a few strokes.

He kneeled in front of me and put his mouth on my core. This made me lay back down on the mattress. He played with my clit while licking my arousal. Then suddenly he clamped down his teeth on my clit and I shredded into a million pieces. He still dint stop and thrust three fingers into me. No warning, no buildup just thrust three fingers in me "Now come Ji Eun" he said. I tried to push him away. "I need a shower, I stink." "Don't fucking care" Ji Hyun said. "Now, I told you to come.' He growled further. At his command I came apart on his fingers. My whole body shaking as my orgasm spiraled through my body.

By the time I came back to planet earth I was in Ji Hyun's arms and he was carrying me to the bathroom to wash up. Once reaching the bathroom he set me down on the floor and adjusted the water temperature. I generally like scalding hot showers but at this point I don't mind anything as long as it is with JH.

In the shower we washed up each other fully. Coming out of it he made quick work of drying s up and moved back to the room. Upon entering the room the humid air coated my body.

I turned around seeing Ji Hyun looking at me. His dark gaze made a shiver run down my spine. In two long strides he was towering me in front of me. He snaked his hand around my waist and pulled me towards him. Our bodies flush against each other's.

We walked towards the bed and on the bed he was on top of me. He kissed me and our tongues fought for dominance and no one was backing off. He bit my lip and I bit back. *Tit for tat.* He smirked a little and again pulled me into a kiss, this time I gave in and let him take control.

"Do I need a condom?" he asked breaking the kiss. "No, I am protected and I am clean." I answered. Saying this he thrust up into me. No lining up, no fingers guiding him in me. He just thrust in me completely filing me, stretching my walls. We both were chasing our high and just as I was about to come apart he pulled out of me, leaving me empty. I groaned at the feeling.

He turned me so that I was now on my belly and entered me without any warning reaching even deeper than before. Soon the fading orgasm was again building up. I felt the familiar knot in the pit of my stomach. "I'm gonna cu—cum" I stuttered. "Let's come together. Hold it" he commanded. After a while it became unbearable and we came together collapsing on the bed.

He supported his weight on his elbows so as not to crush me. He kissed my temple and a tingling sensation ran through my body. No one has ever kissed me on the temple that too with affection. It was every time a kiss driven by lust, not love.

This feeling was way different than before and I wanted to deny that feeling I have for Ji Hyun. I've never felt like this. I never wanted to feel like this. I looked at Ji Hyun to find him looking at me.

"This feeling is new for me too. Don't be scared and just accept it Ji Eun." he said with an uncanny ability to read my mind. He rolled on his side and pulled my body in his embrace and we slept that way. I never cuddled up with my past boyfriends but I liked this feeling of being in a warm embrace. I felt safe. I felt....complete.

I woke up to an empty bed. I found Ji Hyun doing pushups on the floor beside the bed. He was butt naked and his back muscles flexing in all glory as he got down and then pushed himself up. I was just admiring his back body and his taut ass.

He stopped after doing 64 pushups. I was counting involuntarily. He stood up and faced towards me giving me a full view of his naked body. My eyes travelled over his bare body—from his eyes to his lips, to his chiseled chest down to his abs, down the 'v' on his waist and his softened dick and then his thighs and legs. Then my eyes trailed back up and rested on his eyes.

He started doing squats not breaking eye contact with me. He did 100 squats; I was again counting involuntarily, and strolled towards the bed. He pulled me into a kiss, hot and passionate. He reluctantly pulled away from the kiss and left me wanting more. He kept leaving wet kisses onto my jawline to my collarbone and last peck on the lips and said "Good morning, beautiful." "Good morning to you too, hot stuff." I replied. His eyebrows shot up in amusement before a wide grin plastered on his face.

"I am going to shower and then will prepare breakfast, get out of bed sweetheart." He said. No one has ever called me sweetheart moreover it never gave me butterflies. My ears stand up at the mention of shower "Can I join you in the shower?" I asked. He halted in his tracks and turned towards me. "No, we have to plan the day tomorrow and you need energy for that and god Ji Eun, give a man a break." He said before turning around and going inside the bathroom shutting the door behind him.

I pouted a little and got out of bed strutting towards the bag Ji Hyun had brought me of my clothes. He did bring good clothes from my closet along with matching lingerie. I took out a pair on undergarments and clothes.

Ji Hyun came out from the bathroom with a towel around his waist, droplets of water sliding from his chest to his abs and soaking in the towel on his waist. I was literally drooling over this man. "Stop gawking and get freshened up." He said with a smirk.

I picked my clothes and rushed to the bathroom keeping my hand on heart to calm it down a bit. I came out of the bathroom and went out into the hall. I saw Ji Hyun cooking breakfast. He looked at me and asked "pancakes good for you?" I nodded my head and said "Yes" he gave a small smile and got back to cooking pancakes.

We ate the breakfast planning the next day of our escape and talking about random things. I have to say that this man is a great cook. Damn the pancakes were heavenly.

That day went smoothly consisting of some bickering and lots of sex. I was on cloud nine all day. At night we went to sleep in each other's' embrace under the duvet.

Chapter 13-15

CHAPTER 13

JI EUN POV:

I woke up with a thud. I was on the floor beside the bed. "What the fu—mmphf" I was cut off with Ji Hyun's hand over my mouth muffling my words. After removing his hand from my mouth he signaled me to be quite. "There is someone in the house. One of Roth's men." He said and my eyes widened. He took out a gun from under the bed which was taped to the roof of the bed. "Just stay here and don't come out no matter what happens. Understood?" he asked. I nodded and my eyes once flicked to the door and then back to Ji Hyun. He was naked in front of me and my gaze trailed down his body resting on his cock.

I smiled sheepishly and gave a fondle to his balls making him erect. "Shit! Ji Eun. now I have to kill that man with a fucking hard-on. Thank you." he said. "Anytime" Saying this he walked out of the room. There were a sound of a few bullets being shot and then Ji Hyun came back in with a little blood splattered on his torso.

"Have a quick bath. We have to leave as quickly as possible." He said and began packing some things. I walked to him and said "why don't we have one together?" "No Ji Eun we have to go. We don't have time to fuck around." He said sternly making me go in the bathroom with a huff.

I had a quick shower and came out. Ji Hyun was all dressed up in black and ready to leave. I avoided looking at the floor but some blood stains on the wall caught my eye.

We got into the car and backed out of the driveway. "They must have followed us here so we can expect more to come." He stated. I looked back but there was no car that looked suspicious.

After a couple of minutes there was around of bullets and the back window of the car shattered. "Shit!" he muttered. We ducked down as reflex but soon Ji Hyun started firing back at them and I did too. We both had a gun in our hands and Ji Hyun had two more in his vest. Ji Hyun was driving and firing alternatively. I was trying to aim at the car behind us to shoot but as I shot the gun jumped in my hands and it flew in other direction, missing the target widely. I again composed myself, made a tight grip on the gun and fired again this time the bullet made contact with the front windshield and the glass shattered. While looking in the side mirror Ji Hyun shot at them and it hit the tire. The car behind us swiveled to the side and fell off the road.

He took out his phone and threw it into my lap saying "Call Thresh under 'T' and tell him that we're coming in hot." I searched up his name and called him. He picked up on the second ring. "Yes boss?" he said on the other side. "It's Ji Eun this side. Ji Hyun told me to tell you that we are coming in hot. Whatever that means." I said. "How hot?" he asked. "I don't know what that means. I mean, I know I'm pretty hot, both literally and metaphorically--" I was cut off by him "It means you've got pursuit." "Yes there was one car behind us but JH shot them. I can't see any now but they have a knack of showing up when you least expect them." I said. "Tell him I am at the airfield waiting for him" he said and with a click the call ended. "He told me inform you that he is at the airfield" I informed Ji Hyun. "Perfect" he said.

After about half an hour we reached the airfield and there stood a plane. The kind you see in movies about armies. Short size and all grey in color looking like how can a thing like this even fly? Thresh was waiting for us there. He took all the bags from Ji Hyun and hung it over his shoulder, and holy Moses, Thresh was shirtless, wearing nothing but a pair of cut-off cargo shorts, the ends frayed and ragged. He was the most heavily muscled man I'd ever seen.

I stumbled as I passed him, gawking openly. I mean, that kind of build didn't do it for me, sexually speaking, but it was still a hell of an impressive sight. This whole thing didn't go unnoticed by Ji Hyun.

Thresh winked at me. "Take a picture, sweetheart. It'll last longer." "Don't call my woman 'sweetheart,' you big asshole." Ji Hyun snapped. "I'll kick your ass." Thresh glanced from me to Ji Hyun questioning "Your woman?" "You fucking heard me." Ji Hyun said irritated. We boarded the aircraft.

"All right then." He eyed me again, assessing rather than leering. "So, when you say 'your woman', what does that mean, exactly, boss?" Ji Hyun was in the cockpit, flipping switches, settling a headset on his head. He turned around and glanced through the open door. "It means shut the fuck up and mind your own goddamned business, that's what it fucking means."

Thresh's eyebrows rose. "Whoa, dude, Uptight much?" "Uptight?" Ji Hyun rose out of the seat, pulling at the headset. "I'll show you--" "Ji Hyun! Sit down, shut up, and fly the fucking airplane. We don't have time to measure dicks." I snapped at them.

Thresh's eyes, already wide, widened further when Ji Hyun did as I said. The noise of the engines ramped up, and we bolted forward. My eyes widened when I spotted a black SUV on the ramp behind us on the ramp firing at our aircraft. Witnessing this thresh shoved me to one side.

He dropped to his knees, flipped out a bipod and turned on his belly and open fired at the vehicle behind us. He fired in burst of three shots. The banging of the machine gun was the most deafening sound I've ever heard. On the fourth shot the hood of the car crumpled and the entire vehicle flipped forward. Contrary to most movies the car didn't explode in a fiery ball, instead just rocking a few times before coming to a rest.

Thresh calmly folded the bipod, shouldered the huge gun and grabbed a seat near mine. He loomed over me, glanced down at me and winked.

He slammed his palm over a button and the ramp folded up, darkening the interior and removing my view of the ground. "Well that was nerve-wracking." I blurted out. "All in a day's work sweet—I mean Miss Wang." "Ji Eun" I said. "I am sticking with Miss Wang. Ji Hyun can be a vicious son of a bitch." He said.

I wasn't sure what he meant by that, so I just shrugged. "Okay. Well...I'm going up to the cockpit."

Ji Hyun may have been a vicious son of a bitch, but I still felt Thresh's eyes on my ass as I walked forward to the cockpit. I turned and glanced at him, an eyebrow lifted. He just shrugged, making a face that said who, me? I don't know what you're talking about.

I laughed as I took a seat in the co-pilot's chair. "What?" Ji Hyun asked. "Just Thresh. He's funny. I like him." Ji Hyun gave me an odd look. "Thresh is funny, since when?"

I waved it off "So. We're finally going home?" I asked. "Well to the island eventually but our route there will be a little detoured. We are stopping in Miami first, and then to the Bahamas. From there we will be taking a chopper to the island. Gotta make sure we really lost them." He explained.

"Do you think we've lost them?" I asked. He shrugged and said. "I don't know, honestly. I told you I'd never bullshit you, so I won't. You killed his best friend. I don't think we'll ever really lose Roth's guys until Roth is dead."

The rest whole ride was filled with me asking questions about the airplane and which switch does what. We landed in Miami on a deserted airport. Upon asking I got to know it was abandoned a long time ago as a new one opened closer to the main city.

Thresh descended the plane after we did and loaded the bags in a big car and bid his goodbye saying "See you on the docks, boss." With that he took off in the other direction and we sat in the car and drove off out the port and on the roads of Miami.

CHAPTER 14

JI EUN POV:

In Miami we checked into a hotel and booked a room for two night stay. I don't know how Ji Hyun got the currency we are currently using because it is definitely different from the one I used in Brazil.

Our bags were sent to our rooms while we completed the formalities of the check in at the reception. Ji Hyun impressed the receptionist by his charms and lured her into not checking my ID as I didn't have one with me. I was low-key impressed by his new skill I didn't know of.

SMUT WARNING

We entered the room and Ji Hyun pinned me to the wall beside the door and captured my lips in his in a harsh yet hungry kiss. It seemed like he waited for this moment the whole time. "Now that I have you all to myself, I think you deserve a punishment for the little stunt you pulled in Brazil before we had to flee." He said with a devilish smirk reminding me of the incident that he had to kill the intruder with a hard-on because of my horny ass.

I smiled at the memory on which he said "Oh I would love to wipe off that smile off of your face soon baby girl." This being said he carried me to the bed and dropped me on the bed making me bounce once. I looked up at him through my lashes and he looked breath-taking. He pulled his shirt over his head and his muscles flexed with the movement.

I hungrily gawked at his body now a little tanned from the heat. I sat up and worked at his buckle. He stopped me saying "Not so soon, baby girl." This made me furrow my brows in confusion.

He dropped to his knees and slid me on the bed towards the edge and took off my shorts and panties in one swift move and without any warning plunged three fingers deep into me. I lay back down on the bed and the pleasure made me arch my back.

He had no mercy and pumped his finger in and out of me at a fast pace. I felt myself on the edge. I clenched around his fingers and as I was about to explode he pulled out of me and left me hanging. I groaned in frustration.

"Well this is your punishment Ji Eun." he said and again entered three fingers in me pumping in and out. He pressed the pad of his thumb on my clit and moved it in circular motion around my clit bringing me on the edge in mere seconds. He stopped just as I was on the edge.

I was on the verge of my temper. My nerve endings were screaming for release. He started again but this time claiming my ore with his mouth. He was licking me while pumping his fingers in me and his other hand massaging my breast. My hands were in his hair pulling softly on the locks as my pleasure hit me like a freight train and I released my juices around his fingers.

He looked up at me and our eyes locked his chin glistening with my juices. "Do you want my cock Ji Eun?" he asked. I just nodded my head vigorously. "Say it." He said flicking my clit. "Beg for it." "I want it. I want your cock deep in me. Fuck me Ji Hyun." I was not able to complete as he slammed into me. "Ah" I cried out in surprise.

He was thrusting in me at an inhumane pace. My eyes rolled to the back of my head as I screamed through my orgasm. As I returned to planet earth I was flipped on my stomach and was on my all fours. He slammed into me from behind and took my hair into a ponytail in his fist. He felt deeper this way.

I felt myself getting closer to my high and his thrust also became sloppier indicating he was also close. We came at the same time and he flopped on top of me burying me into the mattress.

I was still catching my breath when he got up and made his way to the bathroom and came back with a wet towel and cleaned me up. No one ever did this to me. This feeling was very new for me and I wanted to deny it but I can't.

He cleaned me up with exquisite care like I was made of glass and vanished back into the bathroom. A lone tear rolled down my cheek. He came back out of the bathroom and came near me with a worried expression. "Why are you crying? Did I hurt you?" he asked with concern wiping my tears. I didn't realise that more tears escaped my eyes. I shook my head as a 'no' and looked into his deep orbs.

It felt like he can see through my soul and can guess what turmoil I was having in my head. "Don't be afraid of this feeling Ji Eun. I am feeling the same thing. I was also scared at first but I've come to accept it now." He said with his uncanny ability to answer my thoughts, and placed a small peck on my lips.

Is this the same person who ruined me minutes ago in this same place? How can he change so fast? One minute he was ramming in me like a devil and now talking like an angel. I was surprised at this character change of his.

After-sex talk was never my thing but with Ji Hyun it feels like the sweetest thing to do. Everything is different with him. I've never experienced this. I am scared, I am angry and I am mad at myself for feeling like this.

I pushed these thoughts to the back of my head and lay down on the bed still in his embrace. I went to sleep with jumbled thoughts clouding my mind, the exhaustion of the trip and our hot make out session taking over me. Soon I slipped into a deep slumber and darkness.

CHAPTER 15

JI EUN POV:

I woke up and stretched my hand to the other side of the bed but found it empty. I sat up on the bed and heard the shower running. My eyes flicked towards the bathroom door and minute's later Ji Hyun emerged from there.

"You woke up?" he asked "You were looking so exhausted so I didn't wake you up" "What time is it?" I asked. "It's almost dinner time and I am taking you out for dinner so get up and get ready." He replied. I got up from the bed and got into the shower to wash up.

I got out of bathroom to find a fancy dress on the bed with a set of black lacy lingerie beside it. It had a note saying;

> *Wear this dress and come downstairs*
> *I am waiting for you at the reception.*
> *-JH*

I smiled with the note in my hand and started getting ready. Five minutes later I reached at the reception and my jaw dropped seeing Ji Hyun in a suit. He was looking hot and mouth-watering. I caught the receptionist eying him from the corner of my eye but I ignored her and walked towards him.

"I am glad the dress fit you. Do you like it?" he asked. I shook my head and said "I loved it. How did you get it?" I asked. He smiled saying "I have my ways. Now shall we?" he said taking my hand in his and walking out of the hotel in to the car and off to I don't know where.

"You are looking beautiful Ji Eun." he said driving. "Thank you. You are also looking handsome." I replied. His soft smile changed into a smirk and he said "I can't wait to rip this dress off of you." There he is again going from north to south in a nanosecond.

He stopped the car near a beach and we walked towards the sand. I took off my sandals and was now walking barefoot feeling the warm sand under my feet. There was a table set for two at a few distance and Ji Hyun led me to it. Like a gentleman he pulled out a chair for me and made me sit on it and took his position across from me.

The menu was set and it was served as soon as we sat on the table. I loved his choice of food. Sirloin steak cooked medium, béarnaise sauce with fries and some green vegetables with wine, Barossa Valley Shiraz. The food was exquisite and mouth-watering and we dug in the food.

We ate in silence for a few minutes, the occasional slapping of the waves on the shore being the only sound. We never broke eye contact the whole meal. I was the first to look away from his piercing gaze "the food is delicious." I said. "I'm glad you liked my choice." He replied. After finishing the food, the desert was served. We soon finished the desert also.

"Would you like a walk?" Ji Hyun asked. "Sure" I said. He took my hand in his and we walked towards the sea. In the darkness of the night we walked beside the sea, the waves occasionally touching our feet. I just wished for the time to stop there only.

I was very happy and overwhelmed from this feeling. I turned my head to look at Ji Hyun but he was already looking at me. Thank god it was dark and he cannot look at my flushed face. "Why are you staring at me?" I asked. "I can't bring myself to look away." He replied. At this my face became redder.

"You gave me a pretty hard time back at the island Ji Eun." he said. I knit my eyebrows in confusion and asked "How so?" I asked. "You used to lounge around all day in those small bikinis at the beach side and I had to just stand there on guard and control myself from throwing those little triangles off your body and take you right then and there." He said. "I used to masturbate thinking about you and trust me it was all better than I ever expected."

"I also touched myself thinking about you Ji Hyun. It was hard for me also." I said and our eyes locked. He leaned forward and placed a small peck on my lips and pulled away reluctantly. Then he said something which I never wanted to hear from anyone. "I love you Ji Eun." he confessed. I never loved anyone and I knew what that feeling was. I never wanted to fall in love but when in that moment when he said that he loved me it felt like the only thing that mattered in the whole world.

"I love you too, Ji Hyun." I replied. He snaked his arms around my waist and turned us around while I squealed. He pulled me into a passionate kiss and my hands travelled to the buttons of his shirt. He stopped my hands and said "we've got to wait till we reach the hotel baby." He said with a smirk and led me back to the table where our shoes were. We put on our shoes and drove towards the hotel.

The whole ride was filled with saying 'I love you' to each other. Then out of the blue I said "Ji Hyun you own my body, my mind and my soul, I belong to you and you own me, I am all yours." The last line came out more seductive than I intended.

He turned the car sharply and parked it behind a dumpster and got off the car. He rounded the hood and came in front of my door, opened it and yanked me out the car and pinned me on the concrete wall of the alley. His hand receiving the harsh blow of the wall rather than my back.

From his free hand he pinned my both hands above my head. "Say that again." He commanded. "Which part?" I asked cockily. "Say that again Ji Eun, you know which part." He said more gruffly. "You own me and my body, Ji Hyun." I said "But only if I get to own you in return."

"I've got you pinned against the wall, you can't escape if you wanted to and you're making demands?" he said. "You've got some serious balls baby." I captured in lower lip into my mouth and bit down hard, hard enough to draw blood. "Say it JH, I need to hear it."

SMUT WARNING

"Guess were not gonna make it to the hotel." He said and hoisted my dress up to my hips and pushed three fingers into me. "I am yours Ji Eun, you own all of me." A wave of satisfaction rushed over me. He started pumping his fingers into me which had me riding the cusp of my orgasm. I clenched around his fingers and he pulled out. I groaned in frustration but that was cut off as he pulled down his zipper and thrust up into me. I was on my tiptoes. He was relentlessly thrusting into me. He was buried balls deep into me lifting me onto my tiptoes.

The back door of a building, a few feet away from us, opened and a man came out. He lit up his cigarette and took a drag, two, and three. I moaned loudly and the man turned towards us. Ji Hyun thrust up into me and I moaned again. "Hey, you can't do this here. God that was ho." The man said. From his free hand Ji Hyun pulled out a gun from his back and pointed it at the man and said "Fuck off!!" The man raised his hands in the air and said "Yes sir, fucking off." Saying this he vanished from where he came. Ji Hyun put the gun back "Now, where was I?" he asked thrusting up into me hitting that sweet spot and I moaned again "Ahh, right there." He said with a smirk and I exploded around him into a million pieces. After a few thrusts he finished off into me, straightened out my dress, put me into the car and drove off to the hotel.

Chapter 16-18

Chapter 16

Our last day at the hotel was filled with saying I love you to each other and having sex.

The next morning we were at the front desk checking out when I got the feeling. I leaned close to Ji Hyun. "Can we stay for a little longer?" I leaned my head against his shoulder. "Please?" He glanced at me as he dug an envelope full of cash out of the backpack he'd bought in with us. "Haven't had enough, huh? Jesus, Ji Eun. We've had sex six times in the last eighteen hours. I've given you at least ten orgasms. Plus, Thresh is waiting at the docks."

The hotel employee counting out the cash Ji Hyun had handed her was trying valiantly not to listen, but was failing, miserably. She was blushing scarlet and eyeing us surreptitiously, and lost count three times. "Ten?" She squeaked. "I don't think I've ever come that many times in my entire life." She clapped her hand over her mouth, mortified. "Oh god, I'm so sorry!"

Ji Hyun just grinned at her. "Then sweetheart, you're not having the right kind of sex." He took his change and winked at her. We walked out of the lobby but I was not feeling very well. I felt that something bad was going to happen. I pushed aside the thoughts and followed Ji Hyun out of the hotel.

As the hotel valet was bringing our car we were talking. I caught a glimpse of a familiar figure over Ji Hyun's shoulder and I froze. It was Roth pointing a gun at Ji Hyun's back. Seeing my frozen state Ji Hyun traced my line of gaze and looked behind him.

Roth shot at Ji Hyun three times and one bullet went through his rib cage, other in is shoulder and one a little lower in his body. Despite all of this Ji Hyun shot at Roth from his gun and shot him in the shoulder and near the heart and then fell to the ground.

A shrill scream pierced through the air around us and that sound was made by me. I took out Ji Hyun's phone and dialed Thresh's number and told him about the situation and to hurry.

With the help of the hotel staff Ji Hyun and Roth, both, were taken to a hospital. Both were in critical condition and taken to the operation theater. I was a crying mess in front of Ji Hyun's room.

After few moments Thresh came there and I narrated the whole scene to him. "I've called and informed Mr. Wang he is coming here and will reach in five hours." He informed me. I just nodded my head and hoped for the best.

Ji Wook and Mia reached the hospital and I ran to hug my brother and I bawled like a baby in his embrace. "Don't worry he has survived worse than this, three bullets can't kill him and moreover Roth is dead now." Ji Wook cooed, while caressing my hair. I wondered how Roth died as he was also brought to the same hospital. "He didn't survive the shot by Ji Hyun." he said answering my thoughts. I was relieved that Roth has died and no more danger is looming above us. Ji Hyun was still under watch. Ji Wook pulled me out of his embrace and held me at an arm's distance, inspecting me.

"Are you hurt somewhere? Did anyone touch you? How did you escape? Did they hurt you or hit you? Are you fine?" Ji Wook bombarded me with different questions. "Stop! I am perfectly fine Ji Wook. They did try to hurt me but I escaped safely." I replied and narrated him the whole scene. He listened to me with rapt attention, his expression changing from hurt to shock to anger in nanoseconds. After gauzing his expression I said "I am not as fragile as you think I am."

As I finished narrating my eyes became watery and he engulfed me in his embrace and a lone tear escaped my eye. I wiped it off saying "Ji Hyun will be okay. Right?" I asked sobbing. "Yes Ji Eun he will be alright." He reassured me.

We sat at the bench outside the OT in complete silence with m in Ji Wook's embrace for the whole time. After a couple of hours a doctor emerged from the room and we got up to ask him about Ji Hyun. "We've taken out the two bullets but the third bullet went through his body and caused the most damage to the left artery and resulted in internal bleeding. It missed the heart by a small distance." The doctor said. "We will watch him for a few hours and then shift him to the ward. His condition is still critical." He continued. My heart dropped at the last sentence. "But he is out of danger." He clarified. I heaved a sigh of relief at his statement and sat back down with my brother.

I woke up when the doctors came out form the room along with Ji Hyun on a stretcher. I approached his body and saw that his face was very pale. My eyes became teary at the sight and then they moved him to the ward room. "He will be asleep for a while. You can meet him when the anesthesia wears off." The doctor informed us and went on his way. We thanked him and sat outside the ward room.

After some time a nurse came out of the ward room and told us that Ji Hyun is awake and we can meet him, but he is still weak. I cannot contain my happiness and rushed into the room and saw him lying on the bed in the far end of the room.

I took trembling slow steps towards his bed and saw his pale face. A gasp escaped my mouth. I clasped my hand over my mouth to muffle a sob. A hand caressed my arm and I saw behind me to find my brother supporting me.

Ji Hyun opened his eyes and looked at me mumbling a small 'hi'. He tried to lift his hand but it fell back down on the bed.

I sat beside his bed and took his hand in mine and occasionally graced my thumb over his knuckles.

My brother made arrangements to move Ji Hyun to a VIP room. Ji Hyun was reluctant at first but after I butted in and convinced him, he finally gave up.

CHAPTER 17

JI EUN POV:

Ji Hyun was in the hospital for the past couple of the days. He was elated and relaxed when informed that Roth has died. He was super excited knowing that he fired the bullet which killed Roth.

He was recovering well and the doctors said that he was rather recovering fast. I always stayed by his side in his room, we both stealing glances at each other to stay discreet from my brother.

I decided to tell my brother but Ji Hyun was a little hesitant as in a way Ji Wook is still his boss and my brother will not like the idea of Ji Hyun fucking his little sister so I also dropped the idea.

We steeled a few touches and kisses here and there when my brother was not around.

I went home and knocked on my brother's office door. I went in after he said a small 'come in'. I entered his office and took a seat in front of his desk. I was super nervous about telling him about my relationship with Ji Hyun. I could not look him in the eye. I was fumbling with my fingers, knotted in my lap.

I mustered up my courage and took a deep breath saying "I want to tell you something" "Yeah, go ahead." He said. "I am in a relationship with Ji Hyun, we both love each other and I want you to approve it." I said in one go.

My brother froze and looked up at me. I still had my gaze on the knotted fingers in my lap. I slowly looked up to meet my brothers' eyes and found him smirking. Why was he smirking?

"Took you long enough to tell me" he said and went back to typing on his computer. *He knew. How? How long?* A millions of questions were running through my head.

"You think I didn't notice the naughty glances you throw at each other in the hospital room. The way you look at each other and the few kisses you shared when you *thought* that I was not around?" he asked answering my thoughts.

"You approve of it?" I asked hesitantly. He went quite for a while and then spoke "Yeah, I am fine with it as long as you are happy." he said.

I was elated with the news but my brother told me not to tell it to Ji Hyun as he wanted to know as to when Ji Hyun was going to convey the news to him.

I accepted his request and kept my mouth shut.

I couldn't hide my smile upon reaching the hospital. The doctors told us that he can be discharged after a few days and should rest afterwards. As far as I knew Ji Hyun he will not rest at all and be on duty from day one of being discharged.

I can't help it. It's his choice at the end. Even if I tell him to rest he would sneak out to be on duty. So I did not say anything.

We both were happy with the news of his discharge.

As I was feeding him he was continuously staring at me. "Why are you staring at me?" I asked. "You are just so mesmerizing that I can't help but stare." He replied.

My cheeks heated up and I turned my face away to hide my red cheeks. He held my chin and turned my face towards his and placed a soft peck on my lips and said "I love you Ji Eun. so much that you can't even imagine." "I love you more Ji Hyun." I relied back and pulled him into a kiss.

As I came back home I was greeted by my brother pacing around the living room. I went up to him. As he saw me he said "Oh Ji Eun you came. Sit, I have something to tell you." He made me sit on the sofa and drew in a deep breath and continued "So...um.... I actually... I proposed Mia for marriage and she said yes so I am getting married by the end of this week." He said while rubbing the back of his neck.

I immediately hugged him and congratulated him. I was so happy for him and Mia.

Everything just put into its right place and everyone was finally happy and no more danger looming over us.

Chapter 18

JI WOOK POV:

A knock on my office door interrupted my wayward thoughts. "Come in" I said. Not getting a response from whoever has entered I looked up to see Ji Hyun. He was shuffling from one foot to another indicating he was hesitant. "What has landed you in my office Ji Hyun?" I asked. He took a deep breath and said "I want to ask you something Mr. Wang." He said. "What is it?" I said not looking up from my laptop. "Um… it's that…I love Ji Eun and I want your permission to date her." He said not maintaining eye contact with me. I had an indication from the first day at the island that he likes Ji Eun. He was more than delighted when I made him Ji Eun's bodyguard. Moreover Ji Eun already told me about this.

I stood up from my seat and strode towards him, only a few inches between us, he was looking down not meeting my gaze. I took one step back and said "Okay you have my consent." He looked up at me in pure confusion and I had to hold back my chuckle, a sly smile playing on my lips. "What? It was that easy?" he asked himself but I heard it. "You want me to make it difficult?" I asked smiling. "No, it's just that I thought I had to convince you." He said. "You don't have to convince me Ji Hyun, you saved her putting your life on line and you would do it again if needed. I always knew you liked her." I said. His eyes widened more. "You knew? Since when?" he asked. "The day I made you her bodyguard." I said. "Now, if you ever make her cry I will rip your throat with my own hands. Understood?" "I would expect nothing less. That will never happen or I am sure Ji Eun will do that before you." He said with a laugh and went out of my office. I smiled and went back to my work.

JI EUN POV:

I was meeting Aubrey after so long and without anyone watching us. I narrated her kidnapping in short eliminating my killing someone and mine and Ji Hyun's hot sessions. *Duh.*

She was shocked that the last few days were I was kidnapped and then rescued from there. She asked for all the details and I gave her a tid-bit of what happened. Her wide eyes widened further and she said "Holy hell! You rock girl, you fell in love? With your bodyguard? While you were running for your life? With mafias behind you?" I asked her to shush down so as not to grab attention of the other people. I simply nodded and gave her an invitation card of my brother's wedding. "You have to come and we are going shopping together." I said "As if I would let you go alone." She replied.

On the way back Aubrey said "I thought I could lure Ji Hyun but you hit the jackpot girl." I felt a little jealous but shrugged it off and went on my way.

It was the wedding day of my brother and I was helping Mia in dressing up. Both my brother and Mia were nervous. I was trying to calm Mia down but she was having nothing of it.

I came out of the room and saw Ji Hyun emerging from my brother's room. He came to me and said "You are looking gorgeous baby." He said. I smiled and murmured a 'thank you' to him. "I've never seen your brother this nervous. Not even when we were going on missions." He said.

The wedding ceremony started and I enjoyed the party with my best friend by my side. The vows were exchanging. The whole crowd erupted into a loud round of applause as the couple said 'I do'. The priest continued "Now, you may... ahem" I looked towards the couple as Ji Wook already had Mia tipped back down and kissing the life out of her. I laughed at the scene and went back on talking with Aubrey.

The bouquet throwing was going to happen. Aubrey dragged me towards the crowd of girls standing to catch the bouquet. I scanned the area but couldn't spot Ji Hyun. I stood in the crowd not very excited about catching it. Mia swinged it two times to gain momentum and as she was about to throw it she turned around and gave it to me. I was confused as to what was happening.

She turned me around and my eyes filled with tears. There was Ji Hyun bending on one knee in front of me with a small red velvet box in his hand "Wang Ji Eun. I love you. I want to love, cherish and protect you for the rest of my life. Be mine. Always. Share my life with me. Marry me." he said looking up at me with expectant eyes. I looked over to my brother and found him smiling. *He knew it?* I looked at Aubrey and she was shocked as well as me. I looked back at Ji Hyun and said with tears in my eyes "Yes"

He grins, relieved, and slowly slides the ring on my finger. He stands up and kisses me while twirling me around in his embrace. I didn't even notice that we had a full load of audience who were clapping for us and I become shy and hide my face in Ji Hyun's chest.

"I love you Ji Eun" "I love you too Ji Hyun"

We enjoyed the rest of the party and drank a lot. I was practically drunk and so was Aubrey. We danced and I also had a dance with my brother during which he told me that he planned this entire proposal with Mia and Ji Hyun. I playfully hit him on his chest and smile at him.

As the ceremony ended we retire to our respective rooms and Ji Hyun stays back in my room. We make love the whole night which earns me mischievous glances from my brother, Mia and Aubrey the next morning. I glare at Ji Hyun from across the table and he just grins at me and I melt.

I never thought I would fall in love with anyone but Ji Hyun proved that wrong. Every other day we would sneak out to have fun and till now my brother haven't caught us but if he does one day that day we will see hell.

I love Ji Hyun to the moon and back.

End

Thank you for reading this story till the end. I hope you liked my story.
THE END